shred It up!

by Craig Robert Carey
illustrations by Marty Roper

SALT LAKE 2002

For my shred betties, Karrie and Grace
C.C.

To my relatives in the Northeast, who enjoy
the outdoors all throughout the year
M.R.

Special thanks to Gian Simmen, Erik Brøvig, and Holly Anderson at Santa Cruz Snowboards.

Photo credits: cover, © Ales Fevzer/CORBIS; p. 5, © Brian Bailey/Imagestate; p. 11, © Brian Bailey/Imagestate; p. 17, Allsport USA/Chaun Botterill; pp. 18-19, Jim Gund/Icon SMI; p. 23, Allsport USA/Jamie Squire; p. 24, Allsport USA/Jamie Squire; p. 30, Icon SMI; p. 32, Allsport USA/Nathan Bilow; p. 37, Icon SMI; p. 41, Jim Gund/Icon SMI; p. 42, Icon SMI.

Library of Congress Catalog Card Number: 2001087506

A GOLDEN BOOK · New York
Golden Books Publishing Company, Inc. New York, New York 10106

ISBN: 0-307-26411-4

10 9 8 7 6 5 4 3 2

Contents

1. Shreddin'   1

2. Let the Games Begin   7

3. Going for the Gold!   16

4. Salt Lake City   28

Boardheads, Shred Betties, & Groms 38

1
Shreddin'

Ski season is in full swing and the slopes are packed with people. They all want to try out the new gear they got for Christmas. They zip down the steep slopes. They weave back and forth over the snow. Skiing has been around for a long time. And people love it. They wouldn't change a thing. . . .

But wait a minute—what's that man over *there* doing? He's holding a big, fat ski. It looks like a long skateboard without any wheels. People stop to watch him. Is he going to *ski* down the mountain on that thing?

No! He hops on it like it's a

surfboard. Instead of ski poles, he grabs a rope hooked to the front. Then he rides the board all the way down the slope. Wow!

The man's name is Sherman Poppen. A few weeks before—on Christmas day, 1965—he bolted his two skis together. It was a present for his kids. He invented the snowboard!

Sherman's kids loved their new toy. Sherman wondered if other people would like it, too. He started selling it in stores. He even had a name for the new board—the Snurfer. That's a mix of the words *snow* and *surfer*.

Soon other people saw the Snurfer. They thought of ways to make it even better. Some of them started their own companies, making what they called "snowboards."

But snowboarding wasn't an instant hit. It was almost twenty years before it became popular. Before the mid-1980s, most people had never heard of it. Ski resorts didn't let snowboards on their slopes. They thought snowboarders were rowdy and rude. They thought this new sport was dangerous.

But after a while, snowboarding became so popular, ski resorts couldn't say no any longer. Now snowboarding is allowed just about everywhere people ski. Many resorts have even built special areas just for freestyle snowboarding.

Jake Burton Carpenter was an early snowboarder. He went to different ski

resorts and showed people how to snowboard. "Once people started riding in resorts and stuff, that opened up just a whole new way for us to grow the sport," Jake says.

It may have taken a while for the sport to catch on, but snowboarding is now the fastest-growing winter sport in the world. It's easy to see why. Snowboarders race down mountain slopes. They do tricks and flips. And best of all, they have a blast shreddin' it up!

2
Let the Games Begin

Snowboards have come a long way since Sherman's days. Those old boards were made from plywood or plastic. They had awkward ropes for steering. Some were even covered with carpet to help riders stay on board! And it was hard to do any tricks on them.

All that has changed.

First, today's snowboards *look* much
cooler. They're sleek and come in
bright colors. They have bindings that
attach the board to the rider's boots.
These bindings let snowboarders do
all their wild moves without the board
flying away.

Modern snowboards are also much faster and easier to ride. Riders can pick the boards that are best for them—there are lots of different shapes and sizes.

Only a few years after the Snurfer hit stores, snowboarders started having competitions. The competitions helped the sport become popular.

These days, there are more snowboarding competitions than ever before. There's the International Snowboard Federation (ISF) World Championships, the U.S. Open, the Winter X Games, the Junior World

Championships, and the Vans Triple Crown, just to name a few!

Of course, the *ultimate* competition for any sport is the Olympic Games. They are held once every four years. Only a few athletes from each country compete. So snowboarders work extra hard for the honor of making their country's team.

But before the *athletes* could qualify for the Olympic Games, the *sport* had to qualify first!

In the Olympic Games, athletes from all over the world compete against each other. A sport has to be played by men in

seventy-five countries, or by women in forty countries, for it to be added to the Olympic Games. And that's not all! The sport also must have an international governing body. That's a group of people who make rules and plan competitions. And there must be a world championship for the sport, too.

So did snowboarding have that many athletes in that many countries all around the world? Actually, no! But because snowboarding became popular so quickly, people wanted it in the Olympic Winter Games.

Most sports can take years and years

to become official Olympic sports.
For their first Olympic Games, they are
exhibition sports. That means they're
on trial. No medals are awarded, but
this trial period gives people an idea
of how the sports would do in the
Olympic Games.

So when was snowboarding an
exhibition sport? It wasn't! It became
an official Olympic sport right away.

The International Snowboard
Federation was less than ten years old.
It didn't have the experience or the
power it needed to get snowboarding
into the Olympic Winter Games. Other

sports have been around longer and *still* aren't Olympic sports. Surfing and golf have a long way to go before they get to the Olympic Games.

The International *Ski* Federation, on the other hand, had a lot of power— and a lot of experience. It decided to bring snowboarding into the Winter Games as a skiing sport. That's like the express route to the Olympic Games!

The snowboarders were thrilled. Their next stop—Nagano, Japan!

3
Going for the Gold!

Snowboarding was an Olympic sport for the first time in 1998. Two events were planned for snowboarders—the giant slalom and the halfpipe.

The slalom comes from a skiing event. In it, boarders follow a course marked by control gates. Control gates are poles stuck into the snow that show the path the boarders must take. The boarders zig and zag around the control gates as fast as they can.

"I do the giant slalom because of the speed," top snowboarder Karine Ruby says. And Karine's right—it's all about speed. Slalom snowboarders reach speeds of 65 miles per hour!

The halfpipe is a long trench. Snowboarders ride up and down the sides, doing tricks to impress the judges. There are hundreds of amazing tricks and moves, each one wilder than the last.

The halfpipe comes straight from skateboarding. A lot of the original snowboarders were skateboarders first. They brought many skateboarding tricks to the slopes. Skiing sure doesn't have anything like the halfpipe!

In the slalom, speed is the most important thing. But to a halfpipe boarder, it's the moves that count. The riders are scored by five different judges. Each judge looks for different things. Some watch for height, landings, or difficulty. One judges the moves. One even judges the boarder's overall "style."

After months of training, the boarders felt ready to face the Olympic judges. They packed their gear and headed to Nagano. The big day had finally arrived. The 1998 Olympic Winter Games were here!

The weather wasn't great. It was
rainy. The snow was mushy. But
nothing could ruin this moment for the
boarders. They were stoked to hit the
slopes and shred the pipes!

It seemed amazing that their sport was in the Olympic Winter Games. It wasn't long ago that boarders weren't even allowed on the mountains. But now they were competing for the first Olympic snowboarding medals *ever!*

Everyone had their favorites for the halfpipe, but the man who won the gold surprised them all. He was Gian Simmen, a Swiss snowboarder. When it was his turn to show the judges his stuff, he gave the best performance of his life.

He did a lot of amazing moves. Some of them had crazy names like "backside indy," "alley oop," and "stale fish grab." And he did them perfectly! Gian won the gold medal. "I can't believe it," Gian said. "I don't know what I did. I've never been riding like that before."

Gian Simmen

Stine Brun Kjeldaas, Nicola Thost, Shannon Dunn

Not everyone could win a medal. But even the snowboarders who didn't get a medal had a great time. So did the fans! Now everybody is looking forward to the 2002 Olympic Winter Games in Salt Lake City, Utah.

1998 Olympic Winter Games
Medal Winners

(Giant Slalom)

Men

MEDAL	ATHLETE	COUNTRY
Gold	Ross Rebagliati	Canada
Silver	Thomas Prugger	Italy
Bronze	Ueli Kestenholz	Switzerland

Women

MEDAL	ATHLETE	COUNTRY
Gold	Karine Ruby	France
Silver	Heidi Renoth	Germany
Bronze	Brigitte Koeck	Austria

1998 Olympic Winter Games
Medal Winners

(Halfpipe)

Men

MEDAL	ATHLETE	COUNTRY
Gold	Gian Simmen	Switzerland
Silver	Daniel Franck	Norway
Bronze	Ross Powers	United States

Women

MEDAL	ATHLETE	COUNTRY
Gold	Nicola Thost	Germany
Silver	Stine Brun Kjeldaas	Norway
Bronze	Shannon Dunn	United States

4
Salt Lake City

So who will win the gold in Salt Lake City? No one knows. There are more great snowboarders now than ever before. Here are just a few to watch.

The Norwegian freestyler Terje Haakonsen (TERR-ye HAW-konn-sunn) didn't go to the 1998 Olympic

Winter Games. But if he competes in the 2002 Winter Games, many think he'll win in the halfpipe.

Terje started snowboarding when he was fifteen years old. He's so famous that he even has a move—the Haakon Flip—named after him. Terje has been the European halfpipe champion five times, and world champion three times. No wonder they call him "the Legend"!

In the women's halfpipe, the gold medal could go to Shannon Dunn. She's already won a bronze medal in the halfpipe at the 1998 Olympic Winter Games, as well as medals at

Shannon Dunn

the 1997 and 1999 X Games. She is also a two-time world halfpipe champion and a two-time U.S. Open snowboarding champion. Shannon teaches snowboarding, too!

Shannon is one of the greatest freestyle snowboarders—male or female. Her radical moves have helped more girls get interested in snowboarding. She even has a kind of snowboard named after her—the Shannon 44!

Ross Powers might also medal in the halfpipe. Ross was snowboarding's first child prodigy. That means he was an amazing snowboarder even when he was a kid. Ross competed in his first U.S. Open when he was only nine years old. His fourth-grade class came to watch him!

Since then, Ross has won a lot of competitions, including three national championships in the halfpipe, two gold

Ross Powers

medals at the 1998 ESPN Winter X Games, a bronze medal at the Olympic Winter Games in 1998, and the U.S. Open halfpipe title. At the Salt Lake City Games, he'll only be twenty-three!

Some of the other medal winners from Nagano might also be back in 2002. Will any of them be champions in Salt Lake City? Gian Simmen sure hopes so! He definitely wants to compete in the Winter Games again.

No matter who wins, it'll be a wild day in the pipe and on the slopes!

And what about other events? Will it just be the slalom and the halfpipe?

Maybe not. Some people think that boardercross should also be included in the next Olympic Winter Games. It could only make the snowboarding competition even more exciting.

In boardercross, six boarders take
to the slopes at the same time. They fly
down a course with jumps, gaps, and
ridges. It's a crazy race to the bottom
of the hill.

Another really popular event is the slopestyle, where a snowboarder runs a course similar to boardercross. But the boarder isn't racing. Instead, he or she is going for the best moves over the entire course.

The 1998 Olympic Winter Games showed the world that snowboarding is a serious sport—seriously *fun*, that is! No matter who got the gold, the sport of snowboarding was the big winner.

More people watched snowboarding during the last Olympic Winter Games than ever before. Maybe some of them will go out and try snowboarding for the first time. Who knows—a kid watching the 2002 Games on TV might be a future gold medalist!

Boardheads, Shred Betties, & Groms

Grom Tommy made his way to the top of the mountain. "Hey," he yelled to a nearby snowboarder. "Hey, boardhead!" he yelled again.

Shred Eddie turned around. "Hey, dude!"

"There's a gnarly shred betty in the halfpipe," Tommy said. "She's goofy, and getting fat boost on her method."

"Oh man!" the other snowboarder said. "Didja see what happened? Some poser flailed down the hill and packed into a pinhead. That's wacked!" Both of them laughed.

Huh? *What* did they just say?

Snowboarders have their own language, or "lingo." They have special names for everything! Can you figure out what Grom Tommy and Shred Eddie were talking about?

Aerial A flip done off the wall of a halfpipe.

Air The height a boarder gets when he does a jump or leap.

Bail To pull out of a move on purpose and fall.

Boardhead A snowboarder.

Boost Really high air off a jump.

Fakie Backwards, as in "riding fakie."

Fat "Big" or "huge." Used to describe a rider's air. Telling a boarder he got "fat air" is a great compliment.

Flail To ride out of control.

Goofy Riding with the right foot forward. (Most people ride with the left foot forward.)

Method Air

Grommet (Grom) A small, young
snowboarder.

Knuckle-grabber A skier's name for a
snowboarder.

Method Air An aerial move. The
snowboarder bends both knees, grabs
the heel edge of the board with his

front hand, then pulls the board level with his head.

Ollie A way to get air on flat ground, with or without a jump, by lifting the front foot, then lifting the rear foot while springing off the tail.

180 Air A half circle in the air. The boarder lands riding fakie. This is one of the first real moves learned by freestyle snowboarders.

Pack To crash or fall.

Pinhead A boarder's name for a skier.

Poser A person pretending to be something he's not.

Rail To make fast, hard turns.

720 Air Two full circles in the air.

720 McTwist A crazy move! The snowboarder approaches the wall riding forward, goes airborne, makes two full turns in a backwards direction with a front flip, and hits the ground riding fakie.

Shred To ride fast and stylishly.

Shred Betty A female snowboarder.

Slam To crash.

Stomp To make a good landing.

360 Air One full circle. The boarder lands riding forward.

Wacked Not good.

Wipeout A good fall.